Long Way from Home

AWARD PONY STORIES

Long Way from Home

...and other pony stories

ROSEMARY SIMMONDS

AWARD PUBLICATIONS

ISBN 0-86163-326-1

Copyright © 1989 Award Publications Limited

First published 1989

Published by Award Publications Limited,
Spring House, Spring Place
Kentish Town, London NW5 3BH

Printed in the GDR

CONTENTS

Robert saw the young brumby among the trees

Long Way From Home

Curious woke as the first warm rays of sunshine gilded his chestnut shoulder. His eyelids flickered. Dark eyes looked out on the world before he lifted his head from the pillow of springy snowgrass and rolled onto his belly. He shook his head so that the black forelock flopped over his eyes.

Last summer's foalish fluff had gone with the growth of his first winter coat. Now, he had a mane and tail designed for shade, for protection from the bitter mountain winds and for the swotting of bothersome flies.

Curious turned his head to look at Mighty, the lead stallion of their small herd and snorted. He had a long way to go before he possessed a thatch of the stallion's proportions. Even now, in midsummer, Mighty's waving locks covered his crest neck completely.

Curious stretched his forelegs in front of him and pushed up from behind to stand upright. Then, he leaned back to stretch like a cat, his head drooping between his knees as he yawned. A final shake of his tangled mane and the day had properly begun.

Curious picked at the grass as he made his way down to the creek. He stepped onto the bed of shingle and sand which had been all water when the herd first found this hanging valley a week ago. There were three foals with the herd this year and they still slept beneath their mothers' legs. By the time the yearlings had drunk their fill the foals were up and their

Long Way From Home

He turned his head to look at his leader

mothers were wandering down to drink with the other mares.

For the yearlings it was time to play. Rebel, as always, began a game by nipping her half-sister, Midnight, sharply on the rump.

The little black yearling laid back her ears, but Rebel was not to be put off. Her mother was the dominant mare of the mob, a position she defended with teeth, heels and a mean temper. Rebel took after her mother, especially when it came to provoking the smaller yearlings.

She trotted by again, swanking past with her tail high, then twisted suddenly, landing two hindfeet on Midnight's shoulder. The black yearling shot after her with ears back. Rebel squealed with delight and Curious and Fleck left the water's edge to join in their bucking and shying.

Rebel could outrun them all, but Curious had more daring. He would jump the creek where the others hesitated, or vanish beneath the

canopy of snowgums. Once, as a foal, he had leapt onto the lower branches of a tree to outwit them. He was too heavy for that now.

Finally, Rebel dropped her head to graze. When Fleck nipped her shoulder, wanting to play on, she laid her ears flat and punched at him with bared teeth. It was a sign the game was over. The other three yearlings dropped their heads and began to pick over the grass. The best of the grazing had gone from the valley and with the stream slowly

11

drying up the grass no longer grew so quickly or so sweet. The flush of spring grass behind them, these wild Australian horses known as *brumbies* were becoming lean and hard again.

Gradually, the mob moved up the eastern slope to a finger of trees under which they took shelter from the midday sun, nodding their heads and flicking their tails to keep away flies. The foals slept. Mares leaned against one another drowsily.

Mighty stood a little apart, watching the valley for signs of danger. When the sun dipped past the zenith and Mighty lead the mares out towards the opposite ridge, Curious followed at a distance as he generally did. Staying close to the treeline, he came upon a small creek of gurgling, splashing water and stopped to poke his nose under the fall.

A short distance upstream, a small wallaby was drinking. It started when Curious raised his head and stared back at the brumby with bright round eyes. Curious pushed his head forward, his nostrils dilating as he breathed in the unusual scent.

The wallaby jumped back and sprang away. Curious thrust in under the snowgums and thornbushes, his inquisitive nature now fully roused. He was well up the steep-sided creek when the wallaby found a break in the undergrowth and vanished with a flip of its long brown tail. Curious pulled a leaf from the closest branch and chewed at it. His ears flicked back and forth but he could not hear the wallaby. The leaf was sharp, not nearly as good as valley grass.

His thoughts now turned to the herd and at once he became anxious. He tried to turn but the gully was too narrow. A stone slipped beneath his black hoofs and skittered away behind him. The fear of being trapped set his muscles shaking and brought a fearful sweat prickling across his shoulders. The bay yearling raised his head and called to the herd with a high-pitched whinny.

His dam, Breeze, called back to him from down in the valley. Her own neigh trembled. Something was upsetting her, something she could not explain to him. Curious sensed the mob's restiveness and was filled with panic. Heedless of the branches tearing at him, or the stones that bruised his legs, he went back on his haunches and scrambled himself around. Then he ran, half galloping and half falling, driven by the instinct to rejoin his herd.

Curious was suddenly panic-stricken at the thought of being trapped

A strange humming filled the sky. Breeze neighed again, insistently. The rest of the herd, wheeled before he reached them and flew down the valley at a gallop. Two helicopters cleared the ridge and swung round overhead, driving the herd at speed.

Curious, the yearling, sped after them. He was sliding on loose stones and ducking his head beneath low branches. When he reached the plain he stretched his neck out and drove his legs as fast as they would go, to fly over the grass like a bright flame.

The helicopters dropped like a pair of giant eagles. Curious tried to call out a warning but the wind blew it back down his throat. The helicopters came down again. A sharp cracking noise like the splitting of dry branches broke across the sky. Three brumbies faltered. The older mare, Tawny, stumbled and then pushed on although she was limping badly. Blackie and Fleck went head over heels, groaning as they crashed onto the hard ground.

The sky crackled again and the brumbies were still.

Curious cried out, forcing his pounding legs to cover more ground, driving his feet faster and faster still. The giant birds swooped again. Mighty and Havoc split the mob between them.

Curious saw his dam wheel off to the left with the stallion and swung over to follow her. Then came the dreaded cracking noise again from one of the helicopters and the grey mare dropped like a stone.

Curious skidded to a halt. Ahead of him, as the dust settled, he saw Breeze lift her head and kick out vainly as she struggled to get to her feet. Curious broke into a trot, calling to her, whinnying as if he was a foal again. Breeze saw him and tried to warn him: *"Run! Run like the wind!"*

Curious hesitated. His instincts told him to remain with the herd, but he could smell her blood and her fear. When the helicopter turned and he heard the grey mare's scream he hesitated no longer. Focusing his eyes on the treeline, Curious ran for his life.

The bay yearling cut his speed only enough to zig-zag between the candlebarks and to avoid fallen branches. His legs no longer seemed to be his own. They were running without him, kept going by the simple need to survive. The trees broke and he galloped on, leaping the creek and bounding from rock to rock through the narrow ravine and out through the pass that led into the next valley. Here, should have been

He saw the mare struggle in vain to get to her feet

Copper King's herd, but the valley was silent and bare. Fear flushed through the yearling's veins and banished the aching in his legs that begged for rest. On and on he raced, heart pounding, hot breath rasping his lungs until at last he came upon a thick forest of mountain ash. Here, he slowed and finally stopped to stand with muscles trembling amid the cloud of steam that rose from his heaving flanks.

Pulling a deep breath out of the air, Curious raised his head enough to peer out between the fluttering leaves. The sky was empty except for the black and white flash of a Kurrawong cruising downwind. The forest talked with the chatter of small birds, the scolding of parrots and the slow rustle of a wombat moving through fallen leaves.

The bay's gaze went out over this unfamiliar territory. A plaintive whinny came from his throat but there was no comforting reply.

Curious took a drink from the first stream he found and then plodded slowly on towards the west. His feet were sore now, so he kept to the soft ground as far as possible. On and on he walked, until he came to a small valley high up on the Kootapa range where the grasses were short and dry.

There, he found a small herd of brumbies and his heart quickened with joy. Calling a hoarse neigh of greeting, Curious trotted down the slope. The mob turned, raising their heads.

Their lead stallion was a stocky, mealy-eyed horse. He came trotting out with his head very high and his action extreme as he threw out his feet. He stopped at the edge of the herd and trumpeted a warning to the alien yearling to get out of his valley.

Curious stopped; his quarters dropped making a spring of his hindlegs as he whinnyed once more for acceptance. The stallion was not to be persuaded and he came at the bay youngster with teeth bared, ears laid back and screaming his anger. Curious did not hang around; he spun on his haunches and made for the woods. The stallion did not follow because he knew there was no need. Curious walked on, his head lowered, his heart heavy and feeling utterly exhausted and lost.

Robert Harper woke with a start and reached under his pillow to silence the alarm clock. His heart thudded and his eyes misted with a fearful excitement. Beyond the window, the first pale fingers of dawn streaked across the sky. He slipped out of bed and pulled on denim jeans and heavy walking boots.

His pack had been loaded the evening before. Now, he checked the contents one last time – a blanket, matches, a torch, billy-can and cup, coffee bags sneaked from the kitchen cupboard, biscuits in sealed cellophane wrappings, hard cheese, a pen knife, maps and (most treasured of all) his great-grandfather's compass.

Robert had no intention of running away completely, just for a few nights. He simply wanted to make it clear to his parents that he was grown up and quite capable of looking after himself.

He had been thinking of running off for some time now, ever since the family had moved from Sydney. He liked Mitchell's Creek as it was up in the mountains, but he was lonely. His mother forbade him to cycle the ten miles into town alone and that left him with only Lydia and baby Barry for company.

If he'd had a horse, then at least that would be something, but his father had refused that too. What was the point, he had said, when they might be moving back to the city in a year's time. They would certainly get a dog because his mother wanted one to make her feel safe. Robert's lips curled. She acted as though they were living in the wilderness of his great-grandfather's pioneering days.

Robert hitched the pack onto his shoulders. He set off down the stairs, testing each one for creaks before putting his full weight upon it. The dog

Robert set off down the stairs, testing each one for creaks

heard him and jumped from its basket to greet him with a wagging tail and yelping bark. Robert quickly dropped some biscuits into the dog's bowl and made his escape through the back door.

In a way, it was the dog that had made him finally decide to go because of what his father had said at the sale the previous afternoon. Then, he had finally realised that he would never have a pony or friends or anything, as long as they were at Mitchell's Creek.

They had gone to the saleyard to meet Mr. Bates and buy the dog from him. That was where Robert had seen the brumbies huddled together in their pen, with white-rimmed eyes and bodies trembling with fear. He had wanted one – wanted them all, if the truth be known. He had tugged his father's arm and asked for one, a black foal with a pretty face and a white star. It would not cost much, he was sure of it.

"We are here for a dog," his father replied, shaking him off.

"Please Pa, when we were in Sydney at the summer show, you said that I could have a horse one day," pleaded Robert.

"It will be years before you can ride it, Bob," said his father, "and you'd have lost interest by then."

Guy Bates overheard this and laughed: "You'll never ride a brumby, boy, because they are untameable. Get yourself a nice stock horse if you want to ride. I have a little mare that would be just the ticket for a child."

"Brumbies are vermin, stealing food

from my cattle and running down fences!" He then raised his stick and shook it in the air so that the whole bunch of brumbies shot across the pen, rattling the steel bars. Robert jumped up to catch the stick and throw it down. "Don't do that!" he shouted.

Mr. Harper caught his son's shoulder and shook him. "You apologise to Mr. Bates at once," he ordered. Robert felt his hackles rise. "I won't!" he said stubbornly. "I won't."

"Robert!" The name rang with warning, but the boy stood his ground, watching his father's face turn red with embarrassment. "If you insist on acting like a child, you can go and wait in the jeep."

So he had gone back and sat through the journey home stone-faced, whilst his father whipped him with words. He knew that the main reason for his Pa's anger was that he had felt shown up. The story was told to his mother and he was made to feel like a small child throwing a tantrum. When he was sent

to his room, he made up his mind to run
away that very night.

So, that was why Robert now found
himself following Mitchell's Creek up
to the broad summer pastures where
cattle grazed in their hundreds,
spreading across the mountain slopes
as red and white daisies might stud a
green meadow. Mitchell's Creek was
high in the mountains and by the end
of the day Robert was up on the rough
land of the snow country.

The sun dipped to meet the horizon of

sharp ridges and turn the landscape golden for a brief moment before dusk descended. He needed to find a place for the night, and quickly.

Soon, Robert's shadow stretched long before him as he gathered wood for a fire. He shivered, partly from cold and partly from a growing uneasiness. He had camped out before with the Junior Scouting Club in Sydney, but that had always been with other boys and a leader amongst them who possessed a two-way radio in case there were any accidents. Here, he was quite alone in this spartan little valley which seemed to be on the roof of the world.

The flames of his small fire brought some comfort. They would keep away snakes and dingos. They warmed his hands and gave him courage enough to go down to the stream and fill his billy-can. Robert crouched by the fast flowing water. He splashed his face clean and then froze. Something large was moving on the opposite bank. He strained his eyes to see, his ears to

Robert felt completely alone and suddenly afraid

hear. Now thoroughly alarmed, he
ran as fast as he could for the safety of
the fire.

A bay yearling brumby stood at the
very edge of the trees, his eyes on the
odd scurrying creature that had raced
up the opposite slope. The brumby had
been scared of this newcomer at first,
especially when it kindled the flames,
but now he saw that the creature was
small and timid. Plucking up his
courage, the brumby ventured down to
the stream and snuffled the ground
where the boy had stood.

A new aroma floated down from the
bubbling billy-can. Curious took a deep
breath and then raised his head,
curling his upper lip back to hold the
air in the pocket of his nostrils so that
he could analyse the smell more
carefully. His stomach rumbled and he
realized the boy was eating. He
returned to the opposite side of the
creek to pull at the sparse grass, all the
while keeping an eye on the boy.

Robert had seen the shadow moving

by the creek and realized with relief that the brumby was still young and small and that it appeared to be alone. He chewed on a hunk of cheese, wondering how the animal had come to be separated from its herd. He felt better for having company on the mountainside and had an idea to show his friendship with the offer of some biscuits.

Hitching the blanket around his shoulders, Robert laid a trail of biscuits from the stream to the campfire then sat down to wait. It did not take the yearling long to find the first offering, to sniff it, to turn it over with his mobile upper lip and then flick it into his mouth. Hunger and loneliness overcame his caution and before he knew it, Curious had reached the edge of the firelight.

The boy spoke to him, reassuring and telling the yearling not to be frightened. Robert explained why he had come to the mountains. He began to think of his family and the worry he would be causing them. He decided that in the morning he would go back and then his eyelids began to droop. He yawned, wrapped the blanket tighter about him and lay down to sleep.

Robert woke early the next morning. The fire had burned out. His legs were stiff with cold. He clapped his arms about his shoulders to warm himself and this sent the startled bay yearling skittering into the trees.

"It's all right!" Robert called. The brumby's muzzle appeared between the leaves, but he did not come out. There were about a dozen biscuits left. Robert split the packet to leave half on the ground, then shrugged the pack onto his shoulders and set off down the valley, eating as he walked.

Immediately the boy had moved away, Curious came out of his hiding place and trotted to the pile of biscuits which he munched greedily. He followed the boy down the mountain, keeping a safe distance from him so that he could flee should the need arise.

Gradually, he ceased to make a dash for the trees when the boy turned to call to him and once he forgot himself so much that he replied with a soft whinny.

When the sound of barking drowned the birdsong and Robert ran forward to be greeted by a leaping dog, Curious ran for cover in a eucalyptus glade. He watched the boy be caught up by his parents and saw the tracker, Ed Seargent, knock back his hat and rub sweat from his brow. Then, his nostrils quivered as he picked up the unmistakeable scent of a horse and he lifted his head to issue a shrill whinny.

Robert turned, pointing to the eucalyptus and talking rapidly. Ed Seargent's horse came out of the shadows to call a greeting.

Cautiously, Curious stepped out of the glade. His coat rippled over tensed muscles. Robert caught the dog's collar and held it back as he watched the yearling pick his way over the grass. The mare whickered a second time and the knot of loneliness loosened from the young brumby's heart.

"How about Bob riding back with me?" Ed Seargent suggested to Mr. Harper. "You two take the jeep down and radio the others we've found him." Robert responded with bright eyes: "Oh, please!" His mother made to stop him, then checked herself. "Are you sure it is no trouble, Mr. Seargent?" she asked.

The stockman smiled. "Belle can cope with the extra weight easily and I reckon that will be the best way to get this yearling down." He ruffled Robert's hair. "That bay colt will make you a fine horse when he's grown." Robert looked to his father, his fingers curling into fists. Would he be like Mr. Bates and frighten the yearling off, calling him vermin?

"Guy Bates has it that brumbies can't be tamed because they are too wild," said Mr. Harper.

"Can be if they are older," Ed agreed, "especially once they've decided on a dislike to man, but they were all trackers' and goldminers' horses once long ago. All horses turn mean if you break them harshly, mean or sullen. When the time comes I'll help the boy break him. Right now, he needs a firm and gentle hand to teach him how to behave. Do you think you could do that, Bob?"

Robert nodded enthusiastically. "I'll sure try!" he promised.

Ed grinned and swung him onto Belle's saddle before mounting in front of him, so that the boy could look back and see the yearling follow them. Curious, for his part, was relieved to belong to a herd again, even if it was a strange one.

Dangerous!

"**W**here do you think you are off to?" Mum asked, catching me just as I was about to sneak out of the back door. "Just to Cath's," I replied, lightly. "Not to the farm?" came Mum's usual question.

"I don't know," I shrugged and tried not to blush. It was only half a lie. I did not know for certain whether we would go round to the farm or not. Since it was only just next door to Cath's house and her Shetland pony was stabled there, it could be more than likely we would go to the farm.

Mum came into the kitchen, hands on hips, her mouth no more than a threadline. "You know I don't like you hanging around there," she said sharply.

My lip began to quiver. A cold shiver ran through me. This was the confrontation I had been trying to avoid.

"Have you been riding those ponies, Tess?" Mum went on.

"Not really," I was able to reply, because I did not call sitting on Hiawatha's back while Cath led him in from the field, actual riding for real.

"So you have!" Mum picked up a tea towel and wrung it in her hands. "I told you not to."

"But Cath doesn't mind . . ." I began.

"I do! It is too dangerous!" exploded Mum.

"It's not!" I argued back. "I only walk. Cath has hold of the reins."

"That's enough, Tess!" Mum said crossly. "You can go upstairs and tidy your room because you are not going

over there today. We have to pick Aunt Doreen up from the station at one, anyway."

"I never have a chance to get a proper ride," I muttered sullenly. My heart ached as I climbed the stairs. It was as if all the words I wanted to fling at my mother were pounding to get out and drown my tears.

It had been like this ever since we moved to Picton last autumn. I had not really thought about ponies much when we lived in the city. There, they

41

belonged to a different world of
orchards, brick stables, the Pony Club
and those rosettes that filled my
bookshelf. Then, I quite suddenly
found myself in Class 3C at Picton
Primary School where three of my
classmates had ponies of their own.

Catherine lived out of town at Picton
Cross, so it was a while before I got to
go over to her house after school and
when I did it was magic! She knew I
liked ponies, so she took me round to
the farm straight away to see Hiawatha,
a skewbald Shetland with a round
tummy and a huge fluffy mane.
"Would you like a ride?" Cath offered
and my heart jumped into my mouth.

It was November then and Hiawatha
had a soft teddy-bear coat to which I
could cling. I scrambled up and dug my
fingers into his mane. When he first
moved, I thought I was going to slide
off, but Cath pushed me back into the
right place and soon my legs felt snug
against his warm sides.

I ran home, bubbling with excitement,

Hiawatha was a skewbald Shetland with a round tummy

and told Mum at once. She went through the roof. I'd never seen her so mad before. You'd have thought I'd announced my plans to become a lion-tamer, or to make friends with a shark, not merely to ask for riding lessons. Perhaps, if there had been a riding school nearby, I could have talked her round. As it was, the nearest approved stable was ten miles away and Mum refused to consider anywhere else.

I was too cross to tidy my room as I had been told and instead curled up on the bed with a pony book and vowed that I would never give in. I wanted riding lessons and if Mum could be stubborn then so could I!

It was some time later that the loudspeaker burped and crackled over the railway station to announce that the train from London would be arriving ten minutes late. I stamped my feet and wandered down the platform. Sometimes you could see gypsy ponies tethered on the rough ground behind the sidings. Meanwhile, brother Nick, who was equally peeved at being dragged off to the station, pestered Mum for some money to work the chocolate machine.

Only Gary and Dad had escaped coming to the station, having left the house with their fishing lines at dawn. Aunt Doreen was Mum's younger sister. She lived in Spain, where she ran a small hotel with her husband. We had been out there a couple of times, but this was the first time I could remember her coming to visit us in England.

Fifteen minutes later the train rattled into the station. Doors swung open and people spilled out onto the platform, chattering, dashing and clutching at cases. There was no mistaking Aunt Doreen. Her face was teak brown and she was wearing sandals, whereas we had only just got out of two pairs of socks. Nicholas and I were introduced and had our hair ruffled. "Haven't they grown!" Aunt Doreen exclaimed, the way adults always do as if growing was something unexpected in children.

"I don't see why we had to come – I've missed the start of the football now," Nick grumbled as we followed their backs to the car. Mum and Aunt Doreen carried on talking all the way home, while Nick and I sat in silence thinking of all the things we would rather be doing. The instant we got back, Nick switched on the television and plonked himself down in front of it looking as though neither earthquake nor flood would move him.

I was not so swift and got collared to show Aunt Doreen to her room. The door to my bedroom, which is directly opposite the stairs, was wide open displaying all my lovely horsy posters and cards. Aunt Doreen let out an "Aha!" when she saw them and said: "I see you take after your mother."

My feet stopped. I blinked. My brain could not understand her words.

Aunt Doreen nodded her head at the posters. "Your mother was nuts about horses when we were kids," she smiled.

"But she hates them!" I exclaimed.

Aunt Doreen's head went back and her brows shot up beneath her hairline.

"She won't even let me ride," I exploded, "never mind have a pony of my own." My curiosity whetted, I pressed on. "Did she really like ponies once?" I asked.

"Of course," laughed Aunt Doreen. "We were in Wolvisborough then though, so there was no question of lessons. Your grandad would never have agreed anyway. He thought horses were something only for the toffs." She paused and pushed me into the bedroom, closing the door behind her.

"Your Mum was a very stubborn child and she was determined to have a ride whatever your grandad said," continued Aunt Doreen. "When we went on the chapel outing to Handale, she and I sneaked away to look for a pony. We found a couple of horses in a field not very far off. They were big, but they seemed so friendly that Elizabeth

Dangerous!

Aunt Doreen pushed me into the bedroom and closed the door

made me hold the head of the smaller one while she clambered up."

"The horse bucked. Your mother flew over its head and knocked herself out. I thought she had killed herself! Off I ran to get our parents, wailing and crying. Well I might because they were livid! Your mother never mentioned horse-riding again. I think she must have had too much of a fright."

"And that's why she won't let me ride?" I asked.

"Maybe . . . maybe," murmured Aunt Doreen.

I leaned forward, resting my chin on my knuckles. "How am I going to get her to see that all horses are not like that?" I pondered out loud. Aunt Doreen turned the door handle as she told me: "I don't know the answer to that, my love, but I do know that if you fight her, she will only be more stubborn."

What was I going to do? I looked out of the window, seeking inspiration in the clouds. Mum had been asking for it really, riding like that without even a halter. Maybe if I could get her to see the difference ... explain how Cath had Hiawatha under control ... how she lent me her riding hat if I rode across the yard ... it was worth a chance!

I intended to introduce the subject of riding tactfully by bringing up the crash helmet Gary had got for his moped, but the words burst out in a torrent of excitement. "You needn't worry about me falling off," I assured her "I always wear a hat and anyway the horse you rode might not even have been broken."

Mum turned round, blinking. "What are you rabbiting on about, Tess?" she demanded.

"Aunt Doreen told me how you fell off and knocked yourself out. You should have had a hard hat on and a saddle and . . . oh, Mum, I wish you'd told me!" I blurted out.

Mum bit her lip. Her fingers plucked the sleeve of her knitted dress. "I couldn't tell you," she said. "I was so scared when it happened. I had dizzy spells for weeks afterwards. I'd forgotten about it until we came here and you started on about ponies. It was stupid of me to try and stop you, I suppose, but I was frightened you might have an accident. Ponies seem such big and rough animals."

"Not when you know them," I soothed her. "Hiawatha's really sweet."

Mum smiled and I felt as though a great weight had been lifted off my shoulders. Then, she crouched down and caught my arms with tight fingers. "I'm sorry I've been so bad tempered with you over this, Tess," she told me. "I should have realized that you wouldn't give up just because I told you to. Look, it is half-term soon, so how would you like to spend it on one of those holidays that gives riding courses for beginners?"

"How did you know about them?" I asked with surprise.

"Who tidies your room?" she laughed.

"Sometimes I can't help but peek inside the magazines you leave strewn around. Now, run along and see what you can find. I'll arrange for you to have a couple of lessons at Mill Stables first, so you don't get too saddle sore."

I flew up the stairs as if I'd sprouted wings. Riding holidays! Mum reading my pony magazines! Anything could happen next – even a pony of my own ... maybe!

The Long Acre

I did not want to cycle down to the Post Office to fetch stamps for my mother. This wasn't because I was lazy (though I had been accused of that from time to time) but because Kathleen McDermott might be there with her pony, Quilty. Quilty was a big, black Connemara pony with tufty feathers around his hoofs and a thick, wavy tail. Unlike the rest of the breed, renowned for their intelligence and docility, Quilty would kick and bite and I tended to put that down to Kathleen.

Her dislike of me started within the first week of our moving to Ballybrood, when I won a china ornament she had wanted, at the village fête. If I had acted with a bit more foresight, I would have given it to her there and then and so perhaps have won myself the friendship of both Kathleen and her pony.

Instead, I took the miniature kitten home and from then on Kathleen decided I was her enemy. Whenever she saw me, she would ride Quilty straight at me and laugh when fear overcame my staunchness and I was forced to jump out of the way.

Thankfully, the Post Office was empty when I arrived on this particular day, and there was no sign of Kathleen. I bought my stamps quickly, agreed with Mrs. Kildare that it was indeed a lovely day and hurried home. The children in the village were not very interested in making friends. In my head I could reason why, but in my heart I was lonely.

If I could have had a pony, it would have helped. Then, I would have had a friend. But neither Mummy nor Daddy would be persuaded. The idea of buying a pony that would only be ridden for three months of the year, when I was home during the holidays, struck them as being rather stupid.

"And who will look after it when you are at school?" Mummy asked when I last brought the subject up. I had sighed and given way. I was not Ann Ellis, with parents who had hunted since the age of three and knew everything there was to know about horses. I had to content myself that my school, Willow House, did have a policy for encouraging its girls to ride once a week at an approved centre.

Before you get the wrong impression that we are swimming in money, as Kathleen and the rest of Ballybrood did when they heard of boarding schools and two cars, I had better explain that my father's job requires him to travel a great deal and to move house frequently. Until last April we resided in Bristol, before that it was Sheffield and before that we were in Germany, which I scarcely remember although it was where I was born.

Mummy decided that neither I, nor my brother John, would learn anything if we were forever changing schools. So, once junior days were behind me, I was sent to Willow House and it was from there I had come home for the school holidays.

A broad verge known as the Long

Whenever I could I stopped to talk to the ponies

Acre ran down the hill from our house to Ballybrood village. This was where our nearest neighbour, Mr. Maguire, grazed his ponies. As usual I jumped off my bicycle and went to pat them. Milady lifted her head and her nostrils flickered with a quiet greeting. Further up, Kilkee called to me and nodded her head for attention. She was quite an old mare. Her brown coat was speckled with white around her nose and flanks and her teeth carried a long, Galvayne's groove the colour of a tea stain.

"There's a girl!" I murmured as I stroked Kilkee's neck and searched my pockets for a mint to give her. I had hoped Mr. Maguire would let me ride the ponies, but he had not been very encouraging and even if he had said "yes" my mother would have stopped it.

Mr. Maguire lived in a droopy-roofed cottage with windows stripped bare of paint by twenty winters and glass so thick with dirt it was a wonder any light passed through it. Mummy

dubbed him an unsavoury character and when I suggested we might put Milly and Killy – as their owner called his two mares – onto our field, she refused point blank and said they were riddled with lice.

This was not true, as whatever conditions Mr. Maguire chose to live in, his two mares were clean and healthy. The only thing they were in need of was a bit of pasture to run on.

Next morning, when I drew the curtains and looked out of the window,

I had to pinch myself to make sure I was not still dreaming. Killy and Milly were in our meadow, working their way across the daisy-studded grass as efficiently as a pair of lawn-mowers. I smiled and went back to bed, glad to think they were getting such a good breakfast.

Daddy was not so pleased. He tried to catch them, but the mares just kicked up their heels and ran to the other end of the field. At quarter-to-ten, Mr. Maguire came strolling up to the kitchen and knocked on the window. "Have you seen my ponies, Mr. Wheatley?" he asked. "Those little beggars from the village have let me darling girls out of the stable, so they have."

Daddy pointed to the field.

"Oh! isn't that a picture now," beamed Mr. Maguire. "Those mares will be thinking they are in heaven."

"Then they are about to come down to earth with a bump," snapped Daddy. "Can you catch them, Mr. Maguire?"

Realizing he was not going to be able to leave the ponies in our field, Mr. Maguire sauntered down the garden. I did not think he would be able to catch the ponies. Daddy had not been able to get within an arm's length of them. Expecting a rodeo, I went to the kitchen door to watch.

Mr. Maguire leaned against the gate and whistled. The mares lifted their heads, gave a little shrug and walked up the field to him. No one else seemed to notice this spectacle, but I knew now that Mr. Maguire could not be as bad as Mummy painted him, or the horses would not have come to him.

The next morning, the mares were in the field again. The day after, it was exactly the same. Mr. Maguire's remarks about the village children lost their humour for Daddy, who declared that the old man was making him into the laughing stock of the village.

On Tuesday morning, Daddy got up early and went down to the field with a bucket of biscuits in his hand. The lure was too much for the ponies to resist. I watched them follow him out of the gate and down the lane, back to Mr. Maguire's yard. Later, the old man came trotting up the lane with his face trembling with emotion and I realized that maybe his stories about the village children were true after all.

"My mares, Mrs. Wheatley, have you seen my girls anywhere?" he pleaded to Mummy.

Mummy shook her head and Mr. Maguire looked quite woe-begone. On

impulse, I rushed outside. "I'll help you look for them, Mr. Maguire," I called. For a moment, I thought he was going to send me back. I knew he thought of me as an English girl with no common sense. However, he changed his mind and set off down the road, allowing me to tag along.

The lane down to Ballybrood was twisty. I kept to the side, but Mr. Maguire wandered crazily down the middle, shaking his fist at the sky and grumbling into his stubbly beard.

The car came out of nowhere. Its brakes squealed. There was a dull thud and Mr. Maguire rolled onto the verge.

"Mr. Maguire!" I yelled, running forward.

Behind me, the car door opened. "I couldn't miss him," the young woman said. "I swerved, but I couldn't miss him."

Mr. Maguire's eyes were open. "My back!" he groaned. "It's my back!" I tried to remember the first aid I had learned at school. The injured person must not be moved – that was very important. "My house is just up the hill," I told the driver. "Go and tell them what has happened. Get my mother to phone for an ambulance."

The young woman nodded, jumped back into the car and backed onto the opposite verge to turn round. "It won't be long," I told Mr. Maguire. "Just try to keep still."

He looked at me oddly, as if he couldn't believe I could be so calm and sensible. "The mares," he murmured."

"The mares ..."

"Don't worry - I will go and find them for you," I smiled. "I'll put them in our field while you are in hospital. Don't worry, they will be all right."

His eyes misted. "You will take care of them for me?" he pleaded.

"I'll be happy to - I love ponies," I assured him.

He managed a little smile and told me I'd find everything I needed in the stable. "Look in the fourth stall," he whispered.

After the ambulance had taken Mr. Maguire to the hospital and Milly and Killy were safely in our field, I went down to Mr. Maguire's stable. Unlike his house, it was spotlessly clean. The first two stalls were set ready to house the ponies overnight. The third was filled with hay, a barrel of barley and grooming tools. In the fourth stall was the ponies' harness for the cart and an old, but well maintained saddle.

Tears filled my eyes as I ran my fingers over the soft leather. "Thank you, Mr. Maguire," I whispered and an hour later riding Milly along the beach, I shouted my gratitude to the wind.

Under Attack

It was a glorious day to start the holidays, quite unlike the usual April which normally had nothing but leaden skies and gardeners complaining about the late frost. Brandysnap had dropped the last of her long winter coat and gleamed like soft gold when I finished grooming her. Over by the gate, Jane tightened Pepper's girth and then swung into the saddle. "Let's go over to Kilton Woods," she suggested. "I haven't been over there for ages."

"It's generally too muddy," I pointed out.

"But it won't be if we go early," Jane persisted, "before the ground gets churned up!"

"Are there any jumps?" Zoe wanted to know. Sunny was her first pony and she was still nervous about what Jane and I thought of as a good ride.

"Nothing you can't lead him round," I assured her.

All three ponies seemed to sense our excitement. They stuck their heads in the air and jogged about. Jogging was normal for Pepper as she's got a bit of Thoroughbred blood in her, but Brandysnap and Sunny were steady natives. Normally, they only got worked up when there was a feed in the offing.

When we touched the broad grass verge that runs the length of Terry Muir's ten-acre field we couldn't stop them. Pepper pranced about like a ping-pong ball and then leapt away at full gallop with Brandysnap and Sunny in hot and lukewarm pursuit respectively.

All three ponies seemed to sense our excitement

We pulled up with a great deal of flourish, feeling breathless and exhilarated by the speed. Even Zoe managed to laugh when she realized she had reached the end of the run safely and in one piece.

I opened the gate from the saddle. Brandysnap is not very accommodating about hinges and latches you have to half fall off to reach. Then, we were off again, trotting along the twisty woodland track. Sunlight shafted between the trees, making golden patches amongst the shadows. Blackthorns were covered in white blossoms, the bluebells had started to push through the grass and bracken, that would make the track impassable come the summer, was just beginning to unfurl.

The way down to the stream was steep and we went in single file. Jane and Pepper went down first, slithering on the mud until they landed with a splosh in the water. Brandysnap took it steadily, planting her big feet firmly

and sliding downwards. On Sunny, Zoe came down last with her eyes tightly shut.

The ponies took a long draught of water. Pepper smacked the water with her forehoof. Brandysnap stood with his nose about an inch above it, pretending to drink so that I would let him stand longer.

Jane led us upstream until she came to a big pool that was swarming with midges. "Yuch!" she exclaimed and clapped her heels into Pepper's sides.

The black pony shot up the bank and flew up the path. Not to be outdone, Brandysnap lurched after her and almost lost me off the back of the saddle. From Zoe's screech, I guessed she had suffered a similar fate on Sunny.

Back along the fields we went on our way home, walking now to cool the ponies' sweating coats. Pepper dropped to roll as soon as she was turned loose, but Brandysnap got straight down to grazing. I could see I was going to have to watch for signs of her picking up laminitis.

She had been bought for me as an early Christmas present and this would be her first spring with me. I had wondered if Mr. Barnes would let me use one of the stables he hired out to hunting horses and light ponies like Pepper, during the winter, so that I could get her off the grass for a bit.

Tuesday proved as glorious as Monday. I walked up to the farm in high spirits, trying to decide whether to ride in the forest or take Brandysnap along the sides of the flood canal. The ponies were down at the bottom of the field, where a lazy stream flowed and the grass was lush. Brandysnap lifted her head when I called and then went back to scratching her neck against a fence post.

"You rogue!" I shouted and climbed the gate, hoping she wasn't going to give me a runaround. I caught her easily enough, but she was in a bad temper and kept swishing her tail and shaking her head at me. I put it down to the fact she had been worked four days in a row and promised her Wednesday off. Time did not take long to set me right.

When I called Brandysnap up to the gate on Thursday, she ignored me and continued to scratch against the fence. My heart felt uneasy and I ran down the meadow. The sight that greeted me stopped me in my tracks. Her neck was rubbed raw. Flies buzzed back to the oozing scabs as fast as she flicked them away.

"Brandy! What's happened?" I gasped as I stroked her face and haltered her whilst the tears ran down my cheeks. "Let's get you inside away from the flies?" I put her in one of the boxes and ran over to the farm to call for the local vet.

Mr. Skelton arrived an hour later, by which time I was nearly out of my mind with worry. He looked Brandy over, checked her temperature and the conditions she had been kept in then

Brandysnap was in a dreadful state!

said: "It's sweet itch."

"What?" I asked.

"It's an allergy," Mr. Skelton explained. "It seems to be set off by midge bites." I thought of the swarms we had seen on Kilton Beck and asked: "Can it be cured?" "Not completely," sighed Mr. Skelton. "She will always be susceptible, but you can soothe the itchiness to give the skin a chance to mend. Have you the use of this stable?"

I nodded.

"She will need to be kept in by day," he told me. "Dawn and dusk are the worst times for attacks. When you want to exercise her, make sure you put a fly repellent on her coat and keep the stable scrupulously clean to keep the flies away." He gave me a lotion to treat her with right away and said he would call again in a couple of days to see how I was getting on.

Poor Brandysnap! I would have to stable her permanently over the summer. I knew Mum would never agree to my coming up to the farm at five in the morning to take my pony in and then turn her out again at ten at night.

I pulled Brandysnap's ears gently, "You'll feel better soon," I told her. "And when your skin heals over, we will go on lots of rides to make up for not getting out in the field."

It would be hard work having her in the stable instead of at grass, but I wasn't thinking about that now. All I wanted was to see Brandysnap healthy and happy again.

Too Hot to Handle

My fingers drummed on the white gloss of the windowsill. Where was Mrs. Seamer? If she did not come soon, I would not have time to ride Candy before lunch. Then, at last, a Land Rover turned into Beck Lane. I stood up, almost jumping with excitement and prayed this would not be just another load of sheep for Gunnergate Farm. The Land Rover stopped and I dashed outside.

Mrs. Seamer turned and held out her hand to me, saying: "Margaret Dean, that's right, isn't it?"

I nodded. My legs were trembling. In a moment I would see her. My pony! My very own!

Mrs. Seamer looked doubtfully at the short row of semi-detached houses that made up the south side of the lane. "They have very long gardens," I said hurriedly. "Paddocks, really. We have got everything ready for Candy - a stable, hay, feed . . . all the fences have been checked." Yes, I had done everything I could to fill the last days of waiting, right down to dusting the stable.

The ramp touched the ground and Candy whinnied from inside the trailer.

"Stand clear while I get her out," said Mrs. Seamer.

Candy stamped and snorted and looked about her with big eyes. She sniffed the garden flowers and blew her nostrils into wide rings. Mrs. Seamer took off the bandages and rug she had used for travelling and carried them to the car. "I hope you enjoy her," she called out as she left. "Candy has always been a lovely pony."

Mum came out of the kitchen to have a look at the pony and offer her a carrot. "Don't be out long," she said, when I told her I was going for a ride. It was hard not to. I could have ridden all day. However, I stuck to a short circuit, simply taking Candy up the High Street and back through some fields where I could enjoy a canter.

All too soon we were back home. I turned Candy into the paddock and went to mix her lunch – a whole bucket of chopped apple, horse nuts and oats to make her feel loved in her new home.

Life could not have been happier for me. Every morning I drew the curtains to find Candy waiting at the corner of the paddock. By the time I was dressed, she would be calling for her breakfast. She loved her meals, especially the oats. By the end of the week she was going through all kinds of antics to show her enthusiasm for breakfast.

She began neighing to wake me and when I looked out she would start galloping round the field and bucking in high spirits. She looked terrific.

Having watched her a few times, I decided she would be a winner in the show ring. She had a touch of thoroughbred blood that gave her fine features. Her coat was a very dark bay with black smudges round her eyes and muzzle. I had some money left over from my birthday and I decided to put it towards buying a black show jacket.

In the meantime, I would practise with Candy in the field. I was sure she would look terrific.

The local shows I had been to followed an easy formula. The riders all walked and trotted round together in a circle. Then, the judge would line them up and later they each did an individual show, which seemed to consist of trotting a figure eight, cantering in both directions and then performing a square halt. It should be a doddle.

Candy was all right to school when we were walking, but when I asked her to trot she started pulling at the bit and broke into a canter. Her nose pointed straight in the air. The corners came round alarmingly fast and I stuck my feet out and pulled back with all my strength. Candy bucked, but eventually gave in and I got her back under control. Clearly, she was not very keen on schooling.

Once out of the field, she set off up the High Street at a spanking trot. The

The local shows were always quite easy

moment her feet touched the verge she was off and pulling like a train. She did not stop until we reached the brow of Limekiln Hill. I clapped her neck, the initial panic forgotten in the exhilaration of our gallop.

"That's what you wanted, isn't it?" I told her. "A bit of adventure!" On we went, cantering along the sheep tracks, scattering grouse and lambs, until we came down into Scarthedale and met the road home. Candy was still bouncing when I turned her out afterwards. I hugged her tight, telling her how much I loved her and made sure she had an extra scoop of oats in her evening feed as a reward.

The following morning I woke to the crash of thunder. Candy took her breakfast in the stable and stayed in all day, munching hay while the rain pounded on the stable roof. It was frustrating not be able to ride, but at least I could slip out to the stable with a handful of biscuits and sit with Candy, talking to her and plaiting her mane in anticipation of the shows ahead.

The day after was overcast but dry. As soon as Candy had finished her breakfast, I saddled her up for a ride. She was feeling very frisky and would not stand still for me to mount. She broke into trot without me asking and pulled for her head the whole time. As we approached the cross roads a dog jumped at one of the garden gates. Candy swerved, bucked and broke into a gallop.

Hedges and houses flashed by. I saw cars speeding along the road ahead and I shut my eyes. Brakes squealed, but we were over and pounding up the hill. A rider came into view further up the lane. She saw me and turned her own horse across the road. The strategy worked. Candy skidded to a halt.

"Are you all right?" asked the young woman.

I nodded. I felt hot and cold both at once. Now that it was over, shock hit my legs and they shook against the saddle. Candy brought me back to reality by dancing about and slipping into the ditch.

"She really is full of herself, isn't she," said the woman. "She loves galloping," I explained. "I'm not really used to her yet and she takes me by surprise."

The woman nodded understandingly. "Rambler's been a bit excitable this morning too. He didn't get his ride yesterday because of the rain."She stroked the horse's neck. "He's supposed to be retired into light work now but he can still be a handful when he gets it into his head to gallop, especially if he's got some oats inside him."

"Why oats?" I queried, recalling that
Candy had been eating rather a lot of
them recently.

"They are very heating," explained
the woman.

"Heating?" I felt a fool repeating
everything the woman said, but I did
not understand what she was talking
about.

"Well, they make a horse over
excited, unless he is getting a lot of
work to run it off," she explained. "It's
like over-heated blood or being feverish
I suppose."

"And oats do that?" I stammered.

"Oh, yes!" said the woman as she
stopped her horse. "You haven't been
feeding them to your pony, have you?"
she asked with a sudden flash of
intuition.

I nodded, too embarrassed to speak.

"No wonder you have been having
problems," she smiled. "Don't feed her
any more, not unless she is working
really hard. A couple of kilos of pony
cubes and coarse mix will be all she

needs with plenty of hay."

"Oh!" I responded, feeling an idiot
Worse, I was a complete idiot so far as
ponycare was concerned. I had learned
to *ride* at Trentholme Stables and
thought that was enough.

I rode home with my head bowed. As
soon as I had turned Candy loose, I
collected my birthday money and
cycled into town – not to buy a black
show jacket, but an encyclopedia of
pony management.

If Candy was going to be happy with
me I realized now that it was not just
love she needed, but knowledge.

The Last Time

A wall with rustic poles was the last jump on the course. Sharon Giddings stood in the stirrups, her knees supple, her ankles elastic, taking the shock of each bouncy stride in her legs so that her hands could be firm and steady on the rein. The black pony danced on the spot, gathering her energy and eager for the next jump.

Sharon held her back. "Steady, steady girl!" she whispered. They were facing the obstacle squarely now, three strides out. Sharon leaned forward, loosening the reins and the mare soared over, flicking her feet high behind her to clear the top pole.

Sharon sat down in the saddle, pulling the mare back to a trot. A smile spread across her face. She was the only rider to have gone clear in the jump off. They had won!

Rosettes were awarded. The forty spectators who considered the under-twelve-two jumping worth watching, applauded lustily. Sharon felt her body sway to the rise and fall of her pony's stride. Ebony's hoofs made a soft drumming noise as they cantered round the ring.

The wind on Sharon's face was warm and fresh. She felt satin ribbons flutter against the back of her hand and the scene blurred beyond a veil of tears. This would be the last time.

The exit came round. Sharon brought the mare back to a trot. Behind them, the course was being made ready for the thirteen-two class. Ahead, the showground was busy with horses and

The mare soared over to Sharon's delight!

cattle. Children ran for hot-dogs and Ebony shied at a balloon.

"Hey! Sharon, congratulations!" cried Elaine Duff, trotting from the practice ring. "Will you hold Clint for me while I walk the course?"

Sharon nodded. "How is he going for you now?" she asked.

"Still pulls like a train," panted Elaine. "Horse Trials are more his scene." Elaine jumped to the ground and handed Sharon the reins. "What about you, have you found a replacement for Ebony yet?" she added.

Sharon shook her head, feeling the tears gather once more. Tomorrow, she would be thirteen and over age to enter Ebony in any show ring classes.

Elaine gave her leg a good-natured thump. "Don't hang around," she urged. "No point in wasting time, with the rest of the season ahead. Fiona Bainbridge has a nice mare for sale – bit of a funny colour, but she's a good jumper. Box Hall, on the way into Westdale. Go up and have a look."

Sharon watched her friend jog in the direction of the ring. She wished she could be as practical as Elaine when it came to selling. Elaine had not wept buckets when the time had come round to sell Dainty, or slipped her extra feeds to keep off any feelings of disloyalty to her pony. Sharon reached over to stroke the neck of Elaine's Clint as if she might convince herself that there were other worthwhile ponies in the world besides Ebony.

But Ebony had been her first, she

had become a friend and they had learned so much together. Sharon wished that she would not grow any more and could keep the little black mare for ever. She could still ride her easily now, though jumping was sometimes tricky.

Sadly, the fact was that Ebony had finished growing, whereas she had not. In two years' time, they would look ridiculous together.

No, she had to sell her now – it was the only sensible thing.

When Elaine returned for her pony, Sharon rode back to the trailer. Her mother was drinking coffee from a vacuum flask beaker and she began praising the qualities of a friend's Cocker Spaniel over those of the Labrador that had won first place in the Obedience Class.

"I've mentioned to several people that Ebony is for sale," Mrs. Giddings told her daughter as they journeyed home. "That might bring some interest, especially after you won your class today."

"I guess so," Sharon agreed quietly.

"Don't take it so hard," consoled her mother. "We can't keep Ebony for ever."

"I know," sighed Sharon, "but it hurts to think of losing her. She's been such a good friend."

"The best thing you can do is look towards the future," advised her mother. "The latest issue of *Horse and Hound* is on the back seat. Look through it and see if you can find a pony to catch your eye."

"Elaine mentioned one over at

Westdale – Fiona Bainbridge's pony," Sharon said, trying to sound sensible and grown up about it. "She thought it would suit me. It's a good jumper."

Her mother smiled. "We'll go up and see it tomorrow," she said.

There was a telephone call from someone named Knowles enquiring about Ebony that afternoon. At six o'clock, a red Mercedes pulled into the kerb at the foot of the garden. Sharon twitched the bedroom curtain and peered out from behind.

Mr. Knowles was wearing a suit. His daughter had a round face and a turned up nose. Her tweed jacket looked expensive. She tapped a leather-bound crop against long boots and Sharon felt she disliked her on sight.

All the way to the stables, Sharon tried to put her feeling of dislike behind her, but it stayed. She forced herself to put Ebony through her paces properly and take her over the fallen tree, but all the time she hoped the mare would do something naughty and put Mr.

Knowles off buying.

Julia Knowles fastened the chin-strap of her hard hat as Sharon rode over and dismounted. Julia landed in the saddle with a bump. Ebony's ears flicked and she rolled her eye, wondering what was going on. Julia flapped her legs. "Trot on!" she ordered and the reins slapped against Ebony's dark neck.

Gamely, she jogged across the paddock. Sharon bit her lip and tried not to see how Julia bounced about, or grabbed the mare's neck to steady herself.

Sharon heard her mother singing Ebony's praises and could tell from Mr. Knowles' response that he was impressed with the pony. She hated the thought of him having her. Julia banged about on the saddle and hauled the mare round. Ebony caught Sharon's eye with a worried look and she reacted without a second thought. Her feet carried her across the field at a run. Her hand reached up to pull Julia from the saddle.

"You can't have her!" Sharon shouted to Mr. Knowles. "I won't sell her to you, I don't care how much you offer. Your daughter can't ride!"

Sharon's mother forgave her the outburst much later when Mr. Knowles had been calmed down and left, and Ebony had been turned out in the paddock. "But you must not do it again, Sharon," she scolded. "At least be polite. Ebony has to go to someone – you can't put it off for ever."

"I know. I won't do it again, I promise," said Sharon. However, she dreaded every telephone call that came after that.

The following afternoon, Sharon and her mother went to Westdale. "She's not much in the show ring," Fiona Bainbridge admitted as she led them to the paddock where Pastel was tethered to the fence, "but she is a really good jumper."

As Elaine had earlier suggested, Pastel was not a pretty pony like

Ebony. She had a roman nose and lop ears. Her hoofs were round and well feathered. Her coat was an odd mixture of cream and white patches.

She greeted Sharon with a gentle nudge and the girl's heart turned over. Riding the mare clinched the deal for Sharon. She loved the strong, firm paces and the way Pastel faced a jump. She was strong, but her pulling came from being keen rather than having any temper. "She's lovely," Sharon said, pulling the mare to a breathless halt. "I'd love to have her."

"We have to sell our pony first," Sharon's mother explained. "There is only space for one pony at the farm. If you can hold on to her we would be grateful."

"We'll keep her back for a couple of days," said Fiona, "but if someone else wants her . . ."

No one came to see Ebony the next day, or the one after that and Sharon began to think she would lose Pastel. On Wednesday afternoon, a young girl

Pastel was not exactly a pretty pony!

knocked on the Giddings' front door. "Elain Duff said you have a pony for sale," she said when Sharon came to the door.

Sharon nodded.

"Could I see it?" asked the girl.

"I was just going up to feed her," Sharon told her. "Do you want to come?"

All the way up the lane, Rebecca Hanley (for that was the girl's name) talked about ponies. She had helped at the riding school since she was ten, she told Sharon. When her friends were away on holiday, she looked after their ponies for them. Now, her parents had given in and promised to buy. Her eyes sparkled at the thought of her own pony.

Ebony was waiting at the gate and whinnied when she saw them. Sharon caught her, led her out and then left her to Rebecca to brush her over and tack up whilst she got Ebony's feed ready.

When she came back, the pony was ready and Rebecca had adjusted the stirrups to her own length. She mounted carefully and rode the mare round quietly. When she said she was too nervous to jump the fallen tree in the paddock, Sharon pulled a branch from the woodpile for her to jump.

It wasn't just that she wanted Pastel so much and that Ebony had to be sold for that to happen – no, she could see that Rebecca would care for Ebony and make her a good friend.

As her mother had said, she had to look to the future. For Ebony, that meant finding a good home. For herself, it meant Pastel and the challenge of new competitions in the years ahead.

Pantomime Ponies

Twenty children walked their ponies round the small outdoor school of Longbeacon Stables. Miss Blythe stood in the centre, flanked by two mothers. All three women wore waxed jackets and wellingtons. Their faces were pinched with cold, their hands buried beneath layers of gloves and dug deep into pockets.

Miss Blythe flexed numb toes and decided she had been mad to suggest another pantomime on horseback. Christmas was busy enough without trying to turn children and ponies into an acting troupe. However, when the leaflet from Hollybush Sanctuary came through the door, she had not been able to resist it. Christmas was about giving, she reminded herself as she asked the ride to trot.

Three ponies went on smoothly. Sparrow refused to go faster than a walk, until Laura became red-faced from kicking. Jane Took's skewbald, Minstrel, decided a gallop would be more fun and shot round the ring, setting off the other young ponies.

"All right, everybody walk," Miss Blythe cried out. "Nancy, come into the centre!"

Faces tightened. There were sighs and frowns as Nancy Wright was chosen for the part of Snow White. Her hair wasn't even the right colour, thought Amy Mackintosh. It's because of her pony Silver that they chose her, because Silver is white and part Arab.

Amy felt on the reins and raised her hands to put an arch into the neck of her Shetland mount, Tandy. She knew Miss Blythe would be choosing the pantomime dwarfs next. They were the only other characters who would ride in the show, apart from the Prince of course, but everyone already knew for sure that would be Simon Cartwright.

Miss Blythe called out names and gaps appeared in the ring. Amy's hands grew sticky on the reins as her sister Jenna turned in to the centre. The seventh name was Laura's.

Miss Blythe rubbed her hands. "The rest of you will be animals," she announced. "Put your ponies back in their stables and come over to the school to listen to the story.

"Amy, just a minute," added Miss Blythe and Amy dutifully waited.

"Will Tandy pull that little cart of yours if we lay the bier for Snow White on it, do you think?" was Miss Blythe's question. "I'm sure she will," said Amy.

"Good! That's everything sorted out then," smiled Miss Blythe. "I'll be relying on you to keep the younger children in order, Amy. They'll be playing the parts of woodland animals. Remember, they must not chase the horses, whatever happens. I don't want any accidents like we had last year."

"I'll keep them under control," Amy replied soberly. She felt it was not quite so bad not to be riding if instead she had an important job to do. Later, Miss Blythe gave her a typed out list of lines she had to learn and told her: "You will be the voice of the animals."

Amy began to think it might have been nicer to have a less important part. Even the dwarfs did not have to do anything alone, but if she got her lines muddled it would spoil the pantomime for everyone.

Laura came round to Amy and Jenna's house several times over the next few weeks to have her costume fitted. All the dwarfs were having special jackets made to cover the cushions that would be used to puff out their stomachs. "I shall melt into my jodhpurs with embarrassment," Laura lamented over a chocolate biscuit. "Sparrow hardly moves faster than a plod. I'll have to spend all my time kicking to catch up and everyone will laugh."

"They're supposed to laugh, that's why Miss Blythe picked you to play Dopey," Amy told her.

Jenna sat cross-legged on the floor, wrapping silver paper round a seaside spade. "You need worry," she said. "Tot's never done anything like this

Laura and Amy and Jenna were kept busy preparing for the pantomine

before. What if he gets frightened and bolts!"

"I'll swop if you are scared," Laura offered quickly. "You can ride Sparrow and I'll ride Twiggy instead."

"No thank you," Jenna replied quickly. Laura must think she was mad to imagine she would swop riding her own pony to plod along on Sparrow. Her Tot would be all right on the night, just so long as everyone else was sensible and didn't excite him. Twiggy must stay in reserve.

December slipped by and term came to an end. The last rehearsal was over and the pantomime only hours away. Amy and Jenna were in the stables, wearing scarves over their faces as they brushed dried mud from their ponies' backs. Tot stamped his feet and would not stand still to be groomed.

Something unusual was going on and all the ponies could sense the excitement. They whinnied to one another anxiously.

"The Wicked Queen has come to harm Snow White. We must warn her."

Amy repeated the lines beneath her breath, brushing mechanically until Tandy's russet coat shone. She glanced at her watch, then called to her sister that they ought to go over to the house to wash and change.

"Okay!" Jenna replied. "Just let me oil Tot's feet."

Just then, Laura slipped in to join them in the stable. Her face was like chalk. "Sparrow's lame!" she whispered.

"What!" chorused Amy and Jenna.

"Ssh!" Laura came closer. "Miss Blythe will kill me, but it wasn't my fault. You know how old he is – with the weather going wet the way it did last night, he's stiffened up."

"You only have to move slowly," reminded Jenna.

"Yes, but he's not just slow – he's hobbling," explained Laura. "We don't want the audience to think we are cruel to our ponies. What am I going to do?"

"You'll have to ride Twiggy," suggested Jenna, but Laura groaned for that would make it impossible for her to keep at the back of the dwarfs' line. "You'll have to!" Jenna persisted. "We can't do the pantomime with only six dwarfs."

"Miss Blythe will never agree," moaned Laura. "But she won't know if you don't tell her," carried on Jenna. "Ride Twiggy in at the last minute!"

Laura twisted her hands together worriedly, then nodded her head. "All right then, I'll try it," she decided.

"What did you suggest all that for?" Amy asked her sister when Laura had gone. "Twiggy will set Tot off - you know how they wind each other up." Jenna bit her lip and confessed: "I hadn't thought of that." Suddenly, she wished she had kept her idea to herself. Tot could be dynamite when he got excited.

Amy stood by the door, waiting to go into the school. It was hot and stuffy inside her bluebird costume, yet her feet were cold. She wrapped the fabric wings her mother had made about her shoulders and stamped her feet to keep warm. The bird's head had been borrowed from the store room in the church hall. It smelled of mothballs and old newspaper.

Amy wriggled her nose and prayed she would not get a sneezing attack in the middle of the performance. That would be just too much. The audience would fall off their seats laughing at her.

As Snow White, Nancy rode her white pony into the ring. "Everybody back," ordered one of the helpers. There was a clatter of hoofs and Miss Blythe came up on her black thoroughbred. The mare champed her bit and danced about every time Miss Blythe's long skirt touched her haunches.

The doors opened. Miss Blythe touched her heel to the mare's side and she leapt forward. A gasp went up from the crowd. Amy decided she would like to ride side-saddle one day. Everyone would want her in the pantomime then.

"Get ready dwarfs!" called Mrs. Luce, one of the helpers.

There was a clatter of hoofs and Miss Blythe came up on her black thoroughbred

Jenna looked back over her shoulder. Laura had better not leave it much later. Mrs. Luce was counting heads. "What's happened to Laura?" she said.

"She'll be here in a minute," called Jenna.

Mrs. Luce peeped into the arena. "You'd better start going in," she decided. "I'll give Laura a call." The dwarfs rode into the school singing their song. Jenna listened for Laura coming in behind her and suddenly she was there in a flurry of hoofs and a worried command to Twiggy to slow down. Tot's head went up and he tried to turn round to see what was going on.

Jenna bit her lip. In the crowd she saw faces smiling. She was sure they were laughing at her. Oh, how she wished Laura had been on Sparrow! Tot took advantage of Jenna's lack of concentration and swung round, snorting at Twiggy.

The chestnut pony was trotting on the spot, her eyes bright with excitement. Jenna took a firm hold on the

rein to pull Tot round and he bucked. Then, Twiggy caught hold of her bit and cantered with Laura to the front on the line.

Tot tried to follow, but Jenna held him back until she realized that the cushion was slipping beneath her jacket and she had to take one hand from the reins to hold it. This allowed Tot to circuit the arena at a merry canter and lead the dwarfs out through the door.

Amy had time enough to hear Miss

Blythe wail: "Why does this always happen!" before she was leading the children dressed as animals in to crouch beneath the trees. It was cold, waiting like frozen statues. Then, Miss Blythe rode in, looking so cross she did not need her Wicked Queen make-up.

Amy stood up and winced as her foot cramped and she felt pins and needles prickle up her leg. "The Wicked Queen has come," she shouted to the gallery. "We must warn Snow White!"

Of course, the warning was too late. Snow White bit the poisoned apple and Nancy Wright (as she was) fell back to lie along the grey's saddle, her head above his tail. "Snow White has been poisoned!" Amy shouted. She looked to the entrance. The dwarfs were supposed to come in now and drive the Queen out, but they did not appear.

"Chase me!" Miss Blythe hissed to Amy and the rest of the animals as she trotted past.

"But . . ." Amy blinked, because Miss Blythe had told them precisely *not* to

"Snow White" fell back to lie along the grey's saddle.

chase the horses. However, there was still no sign of the dwarfs. Amy licked her lips and thought up a new line to put in the script. Then, she waved the animals forwards with her blue wings, calling: "We must chase the Wicked Queen from the forest!"

No sooner had the children playing the parts of animals set off, than the dwarfs finally came cantering in. Debbie Grant, the hedgehog, found this much too scary and ran to her mother who was playing an oak tree.

Snow White's pony began to prance around. Nancy tried to sit up, but couldn't manage it and lay there whimpering: "Oh my back, I've bust it!" Amy ran forward to catch the reins and lead Silver out as she had in the rehearsal, only it all happened rather faster.

This was too much for the audience, who finally did as everyone had predicted and almost fell off their seats rolling about with laughter.

Eventually, the arena was emptied.

Nancy was pacified and as Snow White she was put onto the little cart. Mrs. Mackintosh tied white ribbons to Tandy's tail and forelock and handed Amy the reins. Someone caught hold of Twiggy and tried to calm her down.

Amy led the pony and cart through the doors into the arena. The lights along the sides of the school had been dimmed. The younger ponies suddenly found a sense of occasion and Twiggy had agreed to walk instead of jog now that she was no longer at the back of the line. Simon Cartwright, as the prince, trotted in on his pony. Snow White recovered and climbed onto his horse and it was all over.

As the applause lapped around them Amy thought of all the worries she'd had about forgetting her lines, about how Miss Blythe had told them not to chase the horses and then asked them to do just that, and the tears in her sister's eyes when Tot started playing about.

Everything had gone wrong, yet the audience had enjoyed it and in the end that was surely what counted with a pantomime!

No Complaints

"Let's get in some practice for Tunstall Gymkhana before we turn them loose," suggested Sarah, as we rode the ponies side by side along Galley Lane. "Only if we do bending," said Kelly and Sarah groaned. "You only say that because you win every time," she exclaimed. "You ought to practise something at which you are not very good."

"I can't think of anything," replied Kelly, loftily, then squealed as we smacked Pip's rump and chased her down the verge.

There was only one corner of the field flat enough on which to work. Kelly and Lisa chased the other horses off while Sarah and I struggled to pull some sticks out of the hedge. We managed to make up two more or less straight rows.

Kelly and Sarah lined up for the first heat. Lisa stood at one side with me at the other. We had scored a line in the turf and any pony that stepped over had to back up a stride. Kelly's Pip broke twice and ended up a length behind Sarah's piebald Jimmy, but when Lisa shouted "go" he soon shot ahead. Kelly came home first, just as she had known she would.

Now it was down to Lisa and me. I gathered up my Gideon's reins and very carefully brought him towards the line. My hands tightened. Gideon was jumping about like a March hare, eager to be off. Sarah counted us down. I held my breath, listening to the blood pound in my head. Then we were away,

We managed to make up two more or less straight rows for the practise run

weaving between the sticks at a fast canter. Gideon overshot the last marker and skidded as I pulled him round. We had no chance of catching Lisa after that. "Never mind, Prue!" Sarah called to me. "You did really well – put in a bit of practice and you'll beat her on Saturday."

My heart sank as she reminded me what this race we'd just had was all about. A practice for Tunstall Gymkhana, but I would not be going, not to Tunstall or any other gymkhana. I dismounted and unfastened Gideon's girth, feeling all the excitement drain out of me.

"What's up, Prue?" Sarah asked.

"I can't go to the gymkhana," I told her. "Mrs. Bradley won't let me take Gideon. I asked her last night."

"Go anyway!" urged Sarah.

"I daren't," I confessed. "If she found out, she would stop me riding Gideon altogether."

Sarah put her arm around my shoulders. "What a dragon!" she said.

"Cheer up though, because the gym-khana is being held along with the vicarage fête this year and there's going to be extra classes and stalls and hot dogs. It'll be great fun!"

"Oh, I suppose I'll come," I told her as I turned the black pony loose. If only I could take Gideon too, I thought, as I carried his saddle home. I yearned to be like Sarah and Kelly, with a pony of my own ... a pony I could do with whatever I chose. Right now, I'd be full of excitement, imagining the applause and the new rosettes I would be able to add to the board above my bed.

Instead, I was going home to football on the television and my sister's radio blaring from her bedroom. My parents said a pony was too expensive. When I told them it could be sold again, that the money was not lost, they started going on about vet's bills. They seemed to think ponies were permanently lame.

Gideon was a 'loan' pony. His owner, Mrs. Radley, had bought him as a yearling and broken him herself, then taught her son to ride on him. Darren Bradley was now thirteen and when he sat astride Gideon, his feet flapped around the pony's knees. Hayley Bradley, Darren's young sister, was only just five and had no hope of controlling the lively pony.

So, I made up the missing link. I did not own Gideon, but I kept him in shoes and feed and for that could ride him whenever I wanted. It had seemed a perfect arrangement, until I had

asked Mrs. Bradley the classes in which Darren had ridden Gideon. She came down on me like a ton of bricks and made me promise not to take him to the gymkhana. Not even onto the field. She didn't like the idea of gymkhanas at all.

On the morning of Tunstall Gymkhana, I got up at seven and had Gideon ready to ride an hour later. The morning was beautiful. Gideon trotted along with his head up, his small black ears pricked in front of me. Birds sang from the hedgerows and along the moorside white-tailed rabbits, that had stayed out too late, ran for their burrows.

I took Gideon up through the sycamore copse that flanked the farm and out onto the moor where there was an old drove road along which we could canter. With the peat resounding like a drumskin and the fresh wind blowing my hair, I could not have been happier.

At the top of the brow was a cairn and as always I dismounted and put another white stone on the top. Below us, the valley stretched away in a patchwork of green trees, golden wheat fields and wiggling roads that linked the red-roofed towns. Somewhere in the sprawl of Milburn my family would be having breakfast after a Saturday morning lie-in.

Sarah waved me over as soon as I got to the showfield some time later that morning. Her piebald was prancing about like a mad thing. She'd changed her tack, I noticed, and put a kimblewick on instead of his usual snaffle and a standing martingale. Even so, he was proving a handful.

"Come and watch this, Prue!" Sarah called out and led the way to a space in the field where some other ponies were jumping an uprooted tree. "You aren't going over it are you? It's huge!" I gasped.

Sarah laughed. "Just you watch!" she cried.

The piebald took the jump at a gallop and rocketed into the air. Sarah had quite a struggle stopping him before he reached the line of trailers where ponies were being unloaded and saddled. A loudspeaker called for entrants for the Potato Race. Sarah waved to me and cantered over to the ring.

I found a space on the end of a straw bale and sat down to watch. Sarah lost her race, as usual, but Kelly and Lisa got through to the final. That could have been me, I thought. If it wasn't for Mrs. Bradley being such an old groan I might have been in there receiving a rosette.

The girl at the other end of the bale turned to me with a sigh. "Don't you wish you could be in there with them?" she sighed.

"Oh, yes," I replied, my chest tight with injustice.

"Have you got a pony?" asked the girl and I shook my head.

"Neither have I," she said. "I don't know why I come to gymkhanas. I always end up crying when I go home."

I turned, struck by the ache in the girl's voice. "Do you ride?" I asked.

"Once a week," she explained. "I like it best when Miss Laithe takes the class out on a hack. I can pretend I'm on my own pony then. It doesn't work very well though, I never seem to get the same one two weeks running and you can only do what the leader says. We hardly ever get to canter."

She managed to smile. "Still, can't complain," she continued. "Before we moved to the country I didn't ride at all. What about you, do you have riding lessons?"

I hung my head, too ashamed to look her in the eye. After what she had told me how could I complain about Mrs. Bradley? Riding with Sarah and Kelly, who had their own ponies, I had forgotten how lucky I was to have Gideon at all. I really had no complaints.

Only Fools

James Chapman shut the door to the milking parlour and stretched his arms with a long yawn. He squinted to watch the sun rise over Whingroves Hill on what the calender called the first day of spring.

Spring! He laughed and his breath hung on the air like a tiny cloud. His boots crunched the hard frost into flat white prints. The sharp air cut into his cheeks. On the elder tree, that grew out of a crack in the pathway, green buds wished they had not been so eager to burst into life.

Three tabby cats appeared from the hay shed and ran round his feet, giving a good impression of not having been fed for over a week. Beyond them the penned beasts bellowed for him to hurry and fill their barley trough. "All in good time," shouted James, as he did every Saturday morning.

The first animal on his list of priorities was his horse, Endeavour.

The sixteen-hand bay whinnied as James opened the granary door. It shook his head with a show of impatience. For a growing three-year-old, breakfast could never arrive soon enough.

"You're in for a surprise today," James said. He turned to look at the horse and narrowly missed scooping the most insistent tabby into the bucket. "I've found Grandad's breaking bit."

Endeavour whickered as if he understood, but his eyes were on his feed. "It's all bucket-love with you," joked James, as he opened the stable door.

James stayed a moment longer in the stable, ignoring the cats that rubbed against his legs. He had spent ages looking for the breaking bit and then found it quite by accident. Their sheepdog, Meg, had been trying to dig out a rat she had found in the old foaling box which now formed a hay store. James had pulled back some

bales to help her and when the collie jumped in he heard the chink of metal as the breaking keys clattered against the mouthpiece.

The bit was covered in dust and cobwebs and but for the noise he would have missed it. Now, it was clean and hanging on Endeavour's bridle. "Just waiting to be put to use," James murmured.

"Where are you off to?" Mr. Chapman asked when his son got up from the breakfast table.

"I'm going to bridle Endeavour," James told his father. "I told you last night, I've found the breaking bit." James reacted defensively, feeling his stomach tighten, guessing that he was about to be called to help with something else. There was always a 'something else' that needed attention on the farm.

"I need you to help me spread manure on the bottom pasture," said his father.

"Can't it wait?" James protested.

"We won't get another day with the ground as hard as this and you've all afternoon to play about with the horse," insisted his father.

James guessed his father was going to ask for his help on the farms

There was not "all afternoon," because James spent until three o'clock forking straw from the cattle pens into a waiting trailer. Afterwards, he tried to get Endeavour to take the bit, but the horse just bared his teeth and put his head in the air. By then, James felt too tired to fight him.

"You did a grand job helping me out this afternoon," said Mr. Chapman when they gathered round the fire that evening. "I'll give you a hand with that horse tomorrow. We'll have you on his back in no time."

"I only want to bridle him," said James.

"He's strong enough to carry your weight, so what are you waiting for?" said his father. "Great big horse, eating his head off and not doing a stroke of work!"

"He's still young," James protested stubbornly. "Grandad used to wait until they were four. I'm going to do the same. He said they made their height and filled out better if you didn't back them early."

Mr. Chapman shrugged. "Suit yourself," he said, but his manner made it plain he thought James was being soft.

That was going to be the problem. James wished he could be more enthusiastic about his father's help, but he saw it as interference rather than interest.

His father had no idea about handling horses. He prefered tractors and combines, which might break down but never fought back.

James went up to his room and leafed through his scrapbook of Cleveland Bays, all horses his grandfather had bred. There were a few from the early days, when Grandad was a boy and the farm still worked horses on the land. Most started when his grandfather had inherited the place, along with one brood mare that he had registered under the name Runswick Lass.

Soon, there came two mares and around them a string of young stock.

Endeavour was the first horse on the farm in forty years not to be pure Cleveland Bay stock. Thoroughbred blood showed in his fine face and lighter build. Grandfather had Endeavour bred especially for James. They had planned to train him together, slowly and steadily with their sights set on Badminton Horse Trials.

His grandfather's voice still echoed in his head; *"Only fools break horses, James, wise men gentle them."* His

father would never understand that. Suddenly, it seemed very important to James that he saw to Endeavour's training all by himself.

How he was going to keep his father away, now that he had got it into his head to help, was another matter. James brought the cows in and set the milking machine humming next morning with knitted brows. For once, he did not respond to the bellowing of the young bulls and when Endeavour kicked the door to make him hurry the horse received a curt: "You'd do anything to get your breakfast quicker, wouldn't you!"

James froze. *Anything*? Accept a bit, even?

He dropped the bucket outside the stable door and ran for the bridle. When he returned, the horse had his neck craned over the door and was licking his lips. James pushed him back and slipped inside, but left the bucket outside the door.

Endeavour butted to remind him that breakfast was still waiting, but James was ready for him and had the bridle half over the horse's face before he had realized what was going on. As before, Endeavour tried to throw up his head and show his teeth but the aroma of his breakfast was too tantalizing and when he licked his lips James slipped the bit into his mouth.

The keys lay upon the horse's tongue. He played with them inquisitively, then pushed James gently as if to say this was no substitute for

breakfast. James praised him, leaving
him to mouth the bit a few moments
longer, then slipped the bridle free and
brought in the horse's feed.

Later in the morning, when James came out with his father, Endeavour caught the scent of peppermints in his pocket and offered only a token resistance to the bit. While the horse nudged for a reward Mr. Chapman was edging back towards the house, his mind on a mug of tea with his feet on the hearth. "Looks like you won't be needing me after all," he said. "Not if that's all you're doing."

"That's all for today," James replied and knowing he would be left in peace, he smiled. He felt that his grandfather would also have been smiling.

Strange
Miracle

Even to Virginia Wootton's ears, it sounded excessive to say that her future depended upon her horse jumping a painted pole that was no higher off the ground than her own knees. Yet it was true. If the iron grey gelding did not start jumping soon, he would be sold and in the eyes of her father Virginia would have failed as a horsewoman.

Virginia touched her heels to Therapy's sides and trotted him round the paddock. Her outer leg was drawn slightly back, her inner one pressed firmly against the grey horse's ribs making him bend his spine in a long, smooth curve.

Her wrists bent and her legs closed against the girth as she dropped her weight down into the saddle. Therapy slowed, but did not lose impulsion. His hindlegs came under him, shortening his back like a huge compressed spring.

Virginia flexed her wrists and he thrust forward into a lively trot. His flatwork was faultless. If he had just been a bit bigger he could have switched streams and gone over to dressage.

Virginia sighed quietly, for if he hadn't fallen three months ago he would have carried on along the way to becoming a top class showjumper. She had badgered her parents for years with stories of how she wanted to follow Anne Moore, Caroline Bradley and Annette Lewis to stardom and finally they had given in, at least partway.

Her father bought her a four year old iron-grey gelding that cost more than her three previous ponies put together – Therapy. He was to be the test of her promise; ride him to victory at The Northern Counties Show and she could have her wish.

Virginia brought her horse to a halt, took a breath and turned him at the low jump. Three strides later, Therapy stopped. Virginia shortened her reins to keep him facing the jump and drove on with her heels. "It's only tiny," she

151

coaxed. "You could skip over it."

The memory of their last jump, of them both tumbling into plantpots and wooden boxes, blocked out his rider's voice. Therapy threw up his head, fighting for possession of the bit. His back arched and he erupted beneath the saddle in a frenzied panic.

For five minutes, Virginia struggled to get her horse over the fence, but it was hopeless and he was driving himself crazy in his efforts to get away. Virginia turned away onto the lane that would take them to his stable behind the bungalow. Gradually, the grey dropped his head and settled to a walk. Stretching his neck, his breathing slowly became calm again.

Virginia frowned. Months had passed since the fall. His strained tendons had healed and she had made sure with the vet there could be no physical reason for his refusals, but still it went on.

The following morning she woke with a new plan. Therapy did not trust

Therapy turned up his head in a crazy effort to get away

himself over jumps and did not trust
her, but he might place his faith in
another horse. Virginia leapt out of bed
and ran down to the telephone.
"Hello!" Joe Middleton answered her
call sleepily.

"Did I get you out of bed?" laughed
Virginia. "Sorry, Joe - listen, will
Roulette lead Therapy over some little
jumps for me?"

"He's still not jumping then?" said
Joe.

"Not an inch," Virginia told him.

"Come over around eleven and I'll
see if I can help," offered Joe.

Joe had set out three jumps in his
nearby field. All were small and all
used the hedge as a border and a long
pole to funnel the horses into the jump.
Roulette and Therapy puffed and
snorted to each other by way of
introduction and soon settled into
working together.

Virginia kept her horse in close
behind Joe's big mare. When he
glanced back she signalled she was

ready with a nod of her head. Roulette broke into canter. Virginia felt her mount lengthen stride to follow then abruptly slam on the brakes to skid across the soft ground and straight into the jump.

Joe brought Roulette back to a walk. "Do you want me to have a try?" he suggested.

Virginia shook her head. "He just gets worse," she shrugged. "I was hoping to take him by surprise. Thanks anyway, Joe."

She rode home despondent, seeing herself in a future that would tie her to a typewriter instead of a saddle. That had all been part of the agreement with her parents. If she failed, she had to take up a sensible job. If she won at The Northern Counties Show, on a horse she had trained herself, then her parents would support her dream. The bungalow would be sold and they would move out to the coast, to a house with land enough to keep a string of horses.

It all depended upon Therapy recovering his courage. And that called for a miracle!

The gate out of Dunsdale Wood had dropped on its hinges. Grumbling to herself, Virginia dismounted and heaved the gate open. She had better get used to the idea of riding only at weekends. As for Therapy, he would be sold.

Halfway across the field, Therapy's back stiffened. Virginia took up the rein. She looked up and saw the break in the hedge. She saw the bull lower its head to charge. Her mind was suddenly clear. Her senses were diamond sharp. Therapy spun beneath her and made for the woods at full gallop.

Five bars of moss-covered wood loomed before them. Behind them rumbled a thundering mass of muscle and horns. "For God's sake don't stop!" whispered Virginia. "We are jumping for our lives!"

In a split second, the gate flashed beneath them and they were landing amongst the drooping heads of late bluebells. Safe!

Virginia leaned forward to pat the grey's neck and saw her hand was shaking. Therapy jogged, unaware of her reaction, too pleased with his own achievement. When she got him home, Virginia crossed her fingers and rode him successfully over the low fence.

From then on, Virginia was able to prepare for the Northern Counties.

She could not now be complacent, especially not here on the showground. The arena might spark off the fear in Therapy. There was a strain in competitive work that called for calm nerves, for steadiness as well as bravery.

Virginia shortened her reins a fraction, collecting Therapy's canter into a tight, bouncy stride. His ears were pricked. He moved light as a cat, his hoofs picking at the ground. They had jumped clear in the first round, but that had not been against the clock and she had not had to push him.

To be sure of a prize, they needed to

Virginia shortened her reins collecting Therapy's canter into a tight bouncy, stride

go clear and fast. She would have to hope his agility was still there. Virginia took a breath and pushed the horse into the first jump. Up and over they went, fast and sure. They cut their corners, jumped at awkward angles and galloped every distance.

Virginia came into the last upright too short and let the reins slip as Therapy took off vertically. He skewed over, but was clear!

Five minutes later, Virginia was back in the ring smiling as she accepted a red rosette and the winner's cup. The vision of a typewriter faded and in its place stretched a future of painted poles and applause for Therapy and for herself.

Just
in Fun

"Bet you can't throw as far as that horse," Stephen Fuller taunted his older brother. "Easy!" said Neil who gathered snow from the stone wall and shaped it between his palms to form a smooth firm ball. He drew back his arm, measured the distance with his eyes and lurched forward. The snowball flew out of his hand, cut a white line through the frosty air and smacked the pony squarely on her rump, much to the amusement of all four boys.

The mare jumped and trotted away with her head up, snorting. The boys whooped and made snowballs as fast as their hands could work. Neil sent a second zinging through the air to catch the pony's forehead. She gave a queer squeaking neigh and kicked her hindlegs into the air.

More snowballs followed. Few managed a direct hit but it hardly mattered so long as the mare ran this way and that way.

Darren suggested they throw four at once in a line. This was too much for the pony. She galloped round the field, skidding and sending great clods of snow high with her round hooves. Then, one snowball spun through the air and hit her rump. This made her buck and the boys fell against the wall laughing.

Neil Fuller turned away, blowing on his fingers. "Let's go back and I'll get mum to make us some hotdogs," he said. The others followed him, tossing snowballs at cars that passed them,

shouting and laughing their way up the street.

The piebald finally stopped galloping and looked at the wall. Her nostrils snuffed the air where the boys had been. She pawed at the snow with a foreleg then put her head down to pick at the grass beneath. But she was restive and kept looking up. When one of the chickens flew onto the paddock gate she started and jumped sideways.

Barbara Denham stood on the pedals as she turned her bicycle into the farm lane. "Minette!" she called. "Min!"

The mare's head came up, her ears sharp, hocks slightly bent, ready to run. It took a full minute for her head to come down and for her to start towards the gate.

Barbara put her bicycle by the stable and picked up the lead rein from one of the sheds which she liked to call a tack room. Actually, it belonged more to Mr. Marsay's chicken feed sacks and old buckets, than it did her saddle.

Minette was waiting for her a little way from the gate. When Barbara raised her hand to take hold of the halter, she jerked her head back. "Min!" Barbara's voice wobbled. She was very aware of the size of the animal ... how one big hoof could crush her foot ... how a kick would break her leg.

"Min! Put your head down, please," urged Barbara, but the mare stood like a statue, her attention trained on the road. Barbara stood on her tiptoes and managed to clip the rein onto the halter

buckle. She pulled, making for the gate. Suddenly, the mare decided to follow, barged into her and knocked her into the gate post.

"Minette, stop!" cried Barbara, pulling on the rope as effectively as a mouse trying to hold back an elephant as the piebald dragged her slithering over the slushy ground across the yard and into the stable.

Barbara tied her up short and stood back, looking at her. The courage she had nurtured over two months of pony ownership had vanished. Barbara's heart bumped against her ribs. Minette was in a bad temper. Maybe she should leave her ride for today. The mare had been out in the field, so she did not need more exercise.

Barbara clenched her fists to keep her fear in check. She must ride! She must not give in to her terror – all the books said so. Barbara forced herself to go into the tackroom and pick up the dandy brush and Minette's tack. They would go down Bakehouse Lane, Barbara decided as she brushed at Minette's coat. It would be closed to traffic because of the snow, she told herself. It would be safe.

She put the saddle on the piebald's withers and pushed it firmly back to keep the hair lying straight underneath. The girth buckles barely reached the straps when she first tried. Barbara put her head against the panel and pulled with all her might. By the time she had the bridle on, Minette had let out her breath and she could take the girth up another four holes to

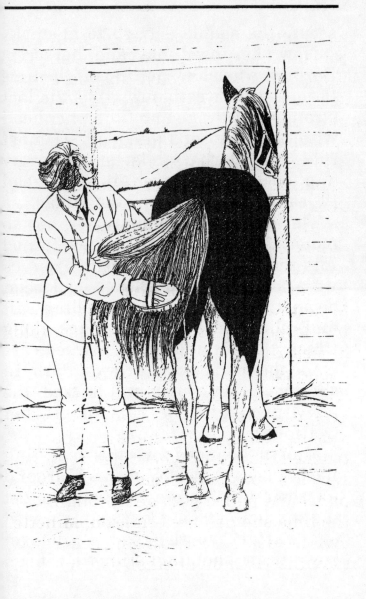

Barbara brushed Minette's coat, deciding where to go

secure the saddle enough to mount.

Now, her hard hat and her crop; Barbara was slow, putting off the time to mount, nerves blotting out the last strands of courage and filling her head with thoughts of falling off. "I must ride her!" Barbara told herself firmly and took the reins over Minette's head to lead the pony out of the stable.

The mare stood quietly for her to mount and, by the time they turned into the High Street, Barbara's nerves were fading. A snowplough had been down the road earlier, spreading salt and piling snow onto the verge along which she normally rode. Parked cars made the road even narrower. Barbara shortened her reins and kicked the pony firmly in the ribs to get her trotting.

Minette bounded forward, unseating Barbara so that she bounced around for some time before managing to get the rhythm of rising and sitting sorted out. Farther up the road a group of boys were shouting. Minette's head came up. Her ears pricked sharply and her stride slowed. A white ball flew through the air and spattered on the tarmac.

Minette stopped abruptly. Barbara lost her balance and fell forward. Next minute, she was hanging onto the saddle with both hands as Minette cantered down the road.

Fear closed Barbara's throat. She could barely breathe. The houses flashed by them. The farm entrance appeared. Minette turned, skidding on the slush. Chickens flew in all directions. Minette shot into her stable and Barbara cried out, ducking her head just in time to miss the lintel.

Barbara slid out of the saddle and leaned against the wall, her legs quivering like jelly. The pony stood at the back of the stable. She held her head high. Her nostrils appeared sucked in and she stared at the door menacingly.

Small hot tears squeezed out from beneath Barbara's eyelids. "You horrible horse, you could have killed me!" She coughed the words out. "I hate you, Minette! I'm never going to ride you again!"

Minette's ears twitched. She spun round, swishing her tail and churning up the straw.

"Don't you dare kick me!" Barbara squealed and ran for the door, bolting it behind her.

Shouts came from the road. Barbara turned in time to see the air erupt with squawking, flapping chickens and

Barbara's legs were like jelly as she leaned against the wall

snowballs. Four boys stood by the paddock wall. "It's not here," she heard one of them say. The tallest boy drew back his arm and sent a snowball skimming through the air. "We can come back tomorrow," he said as they turned away.

Barbara blinked. Snowballs! That was why Minette had been so jumpy.

She ran to the stable and threw her arms round her pony's neck, saying: "Poor Min! - I shouldn't have said I hated you. I thought you were being nasty, but you were just scared, weren't you!" The mare bent her neck to lip Barbara's hand. "I'll try to understand you better," Barbara promised, "and I'll ask Mr. Marsay to put you in a different field, one away from the road."

She rubbed the mare's forehead and realized she was no longer frightened of her. Minette had never intended to kick or bite. She had not meant to knock her into the gate, or scare her by galloping down the street. Barbara rubbed the pony's forehead and reached for the reins. "Let's go and have a nice ride together, just you and me," she said and led Minette out of the stable. "This time it is going to be all right."

Hunter's Moon

"**I** don't want to move," said my younger sister, June, when our car stopped outside a square house with picture windows and walls turned dusty grey with age. When I looked at it and noticed the small *'For Sale'* sign propped against the glass, I agreed with her. However, that was before we went through the iron gate and saw the grassy courtyard with its rose brick outbuildings ... before we heard Dad talk about knocking through shed walls and taking the double doors off the garage . . . before Mum confided her intention of turning the place into a . . . riding stable!

"Really? You really mean it?" I stammered as my most far flung dream showed signs of coming true.

"It won't be easy," Dad said soberly. "It will call for a real family effort."

"We'll do anything you want us to do," June declared enthusiastically.

"I know *you* will," laughed Mum, "but what about Gregg?"

Our eyes all turned to my seventeen-year-old brother. To be honest, I had counted him out of this because his interests did not seem to extend beyond the time when he could afford to buy a sports car. He shuffled his feet now, acutely embarrassed. "There won't just be children coming, will there?" he enquired. "I was thinking if you have adult clients too I might be able to pick up some work."

"There will be plenty work for you," laughed Dad. Gregg, I should add, was an apprentice carpenter. A novice,

June used to call him, as if she was referring to an unproven horse. My sister had a habit of converting everyone into equines. Herself, she saw as a delicate show pony and I was an Appaloosa on account of my freckles.

A month later Maybridge became Hunter's Moon Riding Stable, a transformation sadly lacking in any help from the talents of a Cinderella fairy godmother. We spent every spare hour there – Dad and Gregg worked on the buildings, knocking partition walls down, building, bricking up doorways that were no longer wanted and knocking out holes for new ones.

June and I were banished to the outdoor school, a wasteland the estate agent had called "extensive, cultivated vegetable garden." Within half-an-hour it had reduced June to tears and her heated description was closer to the truth than anything we had read on paper describing the property.

The area we had to tidy was a twenty-by-thirty-stride wilderness of

We spent every spare moment at Hunter's Moon

waist high thistles, stinging nettles and rotting cabbage stalks. It took us three weeks to clear, by which time Gregg had replaced the rickety old fence with new posts and rails and Mum had ordered sand for the riding surface.

Back in the courtyard, the stables were taking shape. When the doors arrived with their proper clip-down bolts, we patted ourselves on the back and toasted the place with lemonade and sparkling wine. Little did we realize how much more lay ahead of us.

The first occupant of the stables was our own Moonshine, a thirteen-hand Connemara mare. Over the last two years, June and I had squabbled almost daily for the best rides on Moonshine and now I was already thinking of her as June's very own. The stable would need horses, and now I rather saw myself on them.

One of the local farmers had a Shetland pony that had been bought for his children and never sold. Mum went to see him and came back leading a pony no bigger than a dog. His name was Tickle.

"You ought to buy something with some blood in it to represent us at local shows," I pointed out to Mum one afternoon as the three of us sat round the kitchen table. My eye was on the photograph of a thoroughbred for sale in *Horse and Hound* – "*Always placed, brilliant across country, school show-jumping team Hickstead last season.*" He sounded perfect.

"Hmmm ..." she replied. Her ballpoint circled an agricultural auction and underlined the word horses. "We'll have to visit the sales and take pot luck," she decided.

"Can we come?" June wanted to know.

"Can you?" she laughed and it was with a light young sound, the way she never used to laugh in our old house when she worked as a boutique manageress in a big department store. "How will I try out the children's ponies if you don't come? Only please, love, don't cry if you see any foals there. Money doesn't grow on trees, you know."

She pulled out a notepad and roughed out her requirements – an eleven-hand f.p. (meaning first pony), a fourteen hand l.w.c. (little-weight-carrier) and a sixteen-hand squiggle which I translated as sensible-adult-ride. Maximum figures were jotted down beside each type. Mentally, I added the numbers and then closed

Mum took us down the lines as she read the catalogue

Horse and Hound with my cheeks burning with disappointment.

The auction was at Throstleby Cattle Mart, an acre of concrete and steel pens. Mum took us down the lines as she read her catalogue, checking certificates and warranties and running her hands over fetlocks and pasterns in what seemed a knowledgeable way, although I'm not sure she really knew what she was looking for.

Mum buys like me, on impulse, on sight. She is rarely disappointed. She is lucky that way. In the course of two hours we had been on the back of every pony in the mart. Many that we would have liked fetched higher prices than we could afford, but we did not come home empty handed.

Within our grasp was a sweet-faced palomino called Periwinkle, a black Dales mare with big round feet and feathers running up her legs as far as the elbow and known as Verity, and an ex-hunt horse with a terrific goose rump called Ryan.

When they had been settled in Mum, June and I stretched out on the garden bench feeling contented and pleased with ourselves. "When do we open?" June asked. "Tomorrow?"

"Goodness, no!" exclaimed Mum. "The horses have to settle in and I have to get a licence. All that will take at least a week to organize."

In fact, it happened a lot sooner than we thought. The Council representative was about to leave for his summer holiday, but promised to fit us in the following afternoon. Mum agreed blithely, then went into a flat spin.

Dad vanished in the direction of Midborough to buy fire-fighting equipment and a first aid kit. The blacksmith appeared to trim feet and slap shoes onto the Dales pony. June took a radio into the tack room and set to work on the saddles we had picked up at the auction while I, with fork and shovel in hand, made my way round the stables.

A little before noon, Mum called us in for a snack lunch and sent me to fetch Gregg from the school. He had finished the fencing and even turned his hand to making three cavaletti.

Before my eyes the scene changed and I saw myself leading a ride on Ryan. I was called into the centre, performing a perfect square halt and the instructress came forward to show everyone the correct position in the saddle.

Instructress! The word rang round my skull like a death knell. Surely Mum had not forgotten to find one?

The speed at which the healthy pink colour left Mum's face told me she had. Beans on toast were forgotten as she flew outside to catch the blacksmith before he left to quiz him for a likely person whom she then rushed after and virtually kidnapped, bringing her to the stables at once.

Our saviour was named Nicola, an immaculately turned out nineteen-year-old with gently curling soft brown hair. June said she was a Lady's Hack, which was quite flattering even though

185

it didn't sound it.

The Council man arrived and was taken in tow by our parents, proudly showing off all the safety work and the sand-laid school. Nicola took charge of the vet. She talked incessantly in a quiet but persuasive voice and managed to stand in front of Ryan's angular rump and muzzle Periwinkle with her hands affectionately when he looked about to nip the vet.

So, Hunter's Moon was granted a licence. Dad popped a bottle of sparkling wine to celebrate and permitted June and I to have a glass each. June took a sip and decided she would rather have coke (she was only nine!). I took my glass into the kitchen with her, pulled out a sketch pad and began to mark out posters to advertise our grand opening.

Between us we managed twelve, all with bright lettering and pictures of horses' heads and riders on hacks in the borders. Though I say so myself, I was rather pleased with them.

The following day June and I set off on our bicycles to all the neighbouring villages and towns, pinning up our posters in the libraries and post offices. We were supposed to open on Saturday morning. That left a week to try out the horses and put in some rudimentary schooling. It was the best week of my life ... nothing but horses and ponies from dawn unto dusk!

By eleven o'clock on Saturday morning the place looked immaculate. The tiled roofs had been cleaned of moss, the rose coloured brickwork re-pointed and the stables painted white with black hinges and bolts. All the horses were groomed to perfection, their coats laid with stable rubbers to make them gleam. Even we humans managed a respectable turnout in jodhpurs and boots whilst Gregg treated us to the sight of a new pair of jeans.

Mum went into the office and opened her pristine desk diary expectantly. Dad mooched about the kitchen touching beakers, checking the tea caddy was full and pinching chocolate-coated biscuits out of the gigantic tin that Mum had bought to go with the refreshments.

The church clock struck the quarter hour and the excitement in our veins slid towards panic. The half-hour rang and then noon. Mum closed the diary and went indoors. Gregg vanished to the bottom of the field. Nicola decided to make a strong pot of tea.

It just so happened that there was a

poster of mine in the kitchen. It also
happened that Nicola glanced at it
whilst waiting for the kettle to boil –
glanced back and walked slowly
towards it with a look of disbelief
spreading over her face.

Next minute, the kettle was whistling
and she had snatched the poster from
its drawing pins and gone marching
into the hall. I set off in pursuit and
caught up with her as she pushed the
offending poster under Mum's nose
and demanded: "Is this the only
publicity you had?"

"There's nothing wrong with the posters!" I shouted.

"There's everything wrong with them," she snapped.

"They show horses," I shouted. "Anyway, what do you know? I got an 'A' for art!"

"There's nothing wrong with the pictures, but they are not good publicity." She ran a hand through her hair trying to calm herself. "Look, Mrs. Carlisle, people these days want to know that the establishment is respectable. They will take one look at these and think it is run by a bunch of kids. We need printed posters and newspaper advertisements, maybe even something in a magazine."

Rather than jump to my defence, Mum nodded. "But it is so expensive," she said woodenly. "I haven't the money to spare – I already owe the blacksmith."

I blinked – all that money, gone already! I remembered the money in my purse under the mattress. "You can have my savings," I said impulsively.

"I couldn't," said Mum and though she tried to push the notes back into my hand, I could see she needed them. The money I was going to use for a double bridle for Moonshine would buy a lot of leaflets.

"I don't want Hunter's Moon to fail," I told Mum, "not after we've all worked so hard."

"We could open in a fortnight," said Nicola. "I'll bring my horse Fillip over and do a jumping display. You could give out raffle tickets as people arrive and offer a free lesson to the winner."

The hollow look went out of Mum's eyes. She rubbed her hands together briskly. "Are we offering Turkish baths, too?" she inquired, glancing at the steam rolling in from the kitchen.

Nicola gave a yelp and ran for the kettle.

We advertised the opening of Hunter's Moon properly, and it was a wonderful day. The sun shone, the horses looked even better than ever and Nicola brought over her lovely Anglo-Arab who was guaranteed to make everyone swoon. Mum's diary slowly began to fill with names and times.

Periwinkle refrained from nipping, the Shetland charmed sweets out of children's pockets and Ryan thought he was at a meet and pricked his ears smartly, looking like a five-year-old again.

That night I lay in bed with my window open, listening to the noise of ponies in the field behind the stables. My eyelids drooped as I let out a long sigh of contentment. This is the life, I thought.